THIS BOOK BELONGS to:

_____

To Deborah, Bruce, Allyn, and Arthur,

who each in their own way helped me find my own true happiness.

Library of Congress Cataloging-in-Publication Data   Santat, Dan.   The Guild of Geniuses /
by Dan Santat.   p. cm.   Summary: Mr. Pip the monkey gets depressed because he does not
think the gift he has for his friend Frederick Lipton, the famous actor, is special enough.
ISBN 978-0-439-43096-8   [1. Friendship—Fiction. 2. Gifts—Fiction. 3. Monkeys—Fiction.]
I. Title.   PZ7.S23817Gu 2004   [E]—dc21   2003007930

10 9 8 7 6 5 4 3 2 1   15 16 17 18 19
Printed in Malaysia   108   This edition first printing, November 2015

The text type is set in 15-point Mrs. Eaves.
The artwork was created using acrylic and mixed media on Bristol paper, a little elbow grease,
and the right side of the brain. Mr. Pip's drawing was contributed by Eric Merrell.
Book design by Dan Santat and David Saylor

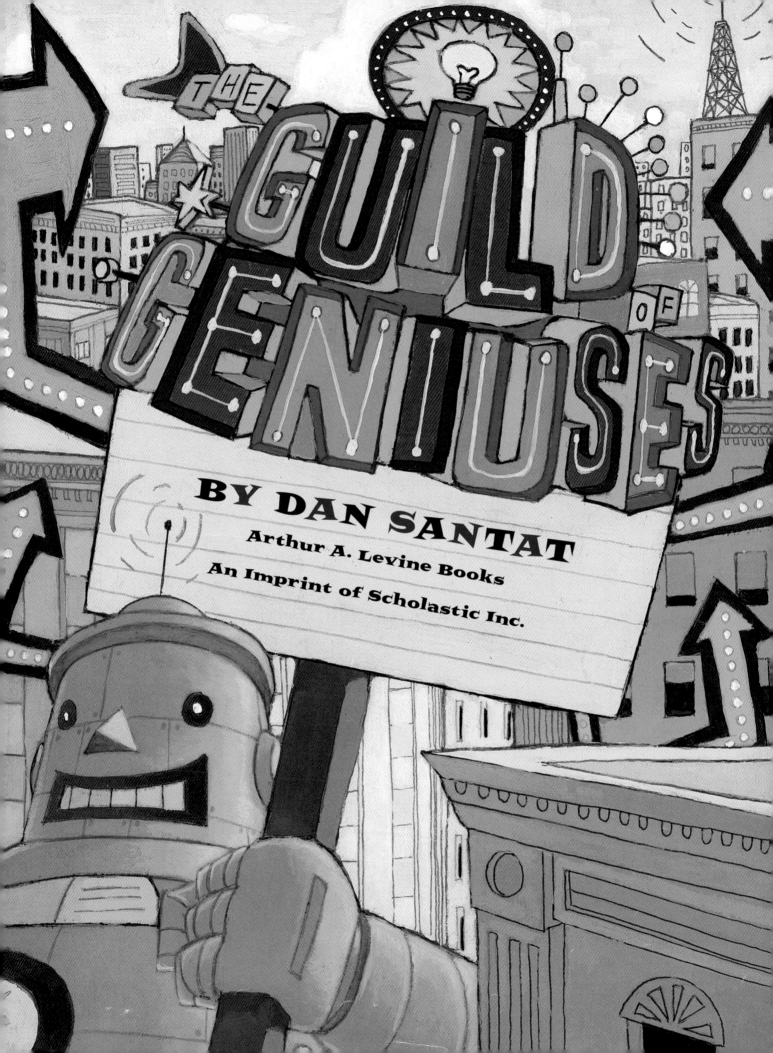

THE GUILD OF GENIUSES

BY DAN SANTAT

Arthur A. Levine Books

An Imprint of Scholastic Inc.

Mr. Pip was best friends with Frederick Lipton, the famous actor.

Every morning, they ate breakfast. Every evening, Mr. Pip practiced different tricks while Frederick studied his movie lines. Sometimes life got hectic, but things usually worked out fine.

On the morning of Frederick's thirty-something birthday,
Mr. Pip jumped out of bed and rushed to give Frederick his gift.

But many gifts from other people had already arrived. The sultan of Brunei gave Frederick a solid-gold car. The president of the United States invited him to dinner at the White House. With all the commotion, there never seemed to be time for Mr. Pip to give Frederick his gift.

The birthday festivities kept Frederick busy, but
every time he saw Mr. Pip, he looked sad.

"What's wrong with you, Mr. Pip?" Frederick asked.
"I've never seen you so miserable."

So Frederick took him to every vet in town.
But each one declared Mr. Pip fit as a fiddle.

"There has to be someone who knows
what to do with you," Frederick despaired.
Then an idea came to him.

Of course! Everyone knew the Guild of Geniuses. It consisted of four of the smartest people in the world, who owned patents on more than ten thousand inventions. There was Dr. Lancaster, inventor of the portable weather machine;

Dr. Monrovia, who built Captain Pong, the Ping-Pong champion and owner of twelve world titles;

and Dr. Torrance, who created the antigravity belt.

Finally, there was Dr. Glendale, who was known for inventing the Greeter.

So Frederick took Mr. Pip down to the Guild and told them
his problem.

"I'll be out of town for two weeks to promote my new movie, but
I'll be back after that. Please help Mr. Pip in any way you can,"
Frederick said. He gave Mr. Pip a quick hug and left.

The geniuses huddled around Mr. Pip and began brainstorming solutions.

"They say music soothes the savage beast," said Dr. Lancaster.

"Maybe the Unmanned One-Man Band can play music that will make him happy again?" said Dr. Glendale.

So they sat Mr. Pip in front of the robot and programmed it to play a beautiful tune.

But it only made Mr. Pip sleepy. "If at first you don't succeed," they all said.

"Perhaps Mr. Pip would like to play with other monkeys,"
said Dr. Glendale.
So they brought some in from Africa.

Unfortunately, Mr. Pip didn't speak
their language, and the only thing the
other monkeys wanted to do was eat
bananas peeled for them by the Robochef.
"Well, that didn't quite go according to
plan," Dr. Lancaster said. "We'll have
to try again."

gemini

aries

pip
major

draco

canis
minor

ursa
minor

pegasus

"Perhaps he wants to feel more important," said Dr.
Monrovia.

So they built a rocket ship and sent Mr. Pip up into
space to be the first monkey on the moon.

When he returned, the city threw him a big parade. "Inconceivable," Dr. Torrance muttered. "Mr. Pip isn't even waving back to the people."

"Back to the drawing board once again," they all groaned.

The end of the two weeks finally came, and Frederick returned. "We're sorry to inform you that we have been stumped by your inquiry," said Dr. Glendale. "This has never happened to us before, but on a positive note, it means you have won a prize!"

Frederick took the prize and was at a loss for words.
But over the silence came some familiar music.

The Unmanned One-Man Band had begun to play "Happy Birthday," while the Robochef brought out a banana-bread birthday cake. With a flourish, Mr. Pip presented Frederick with a gift. Frederick unwrapped a moon rock that Mr. Pip had brought back from his trip into space. Next to it was the picture card that Mr. Pip had made a few weeks earlier.

"A paperweight, how wonderful!" Frederick said. "Even better is this fantastic card! Hey, everyone, look! Isn't this amazing?"

That evening, they all celebrated at the penthouse. "Here's to Mr. Pip," said Frederick. "The best friend a guy ever had!"

Frederick and Mr. Pip made up dances to calypso music. They screeched and sang all kinds of songs. Spending time together was the most fun either had had for weeks. In fact, it was all Mr. Pip had needed in the first place.

It doesn't take a genius to figure that out.

The End